Barbie™
AS
RAPUNZEL

First published in the USA 2002 by Pleasant Company Publications
This edition published in Great Britain 2002
by Egmont Books Limited
239 Kensington High Street, London W8 6SA

ISBN 1 4052 0288 2
Printed in Great Britain
5 7 9 10 8 6 4

FROM THE ORIGINAL SCREENPLAY BY

CLIFF RUBY & ELANA LESSER

BASED ON THE CLASSIC TALE BY

THE BROTHERS GRIMM

ILLUSTRATED BY

ROBERT SAUBER

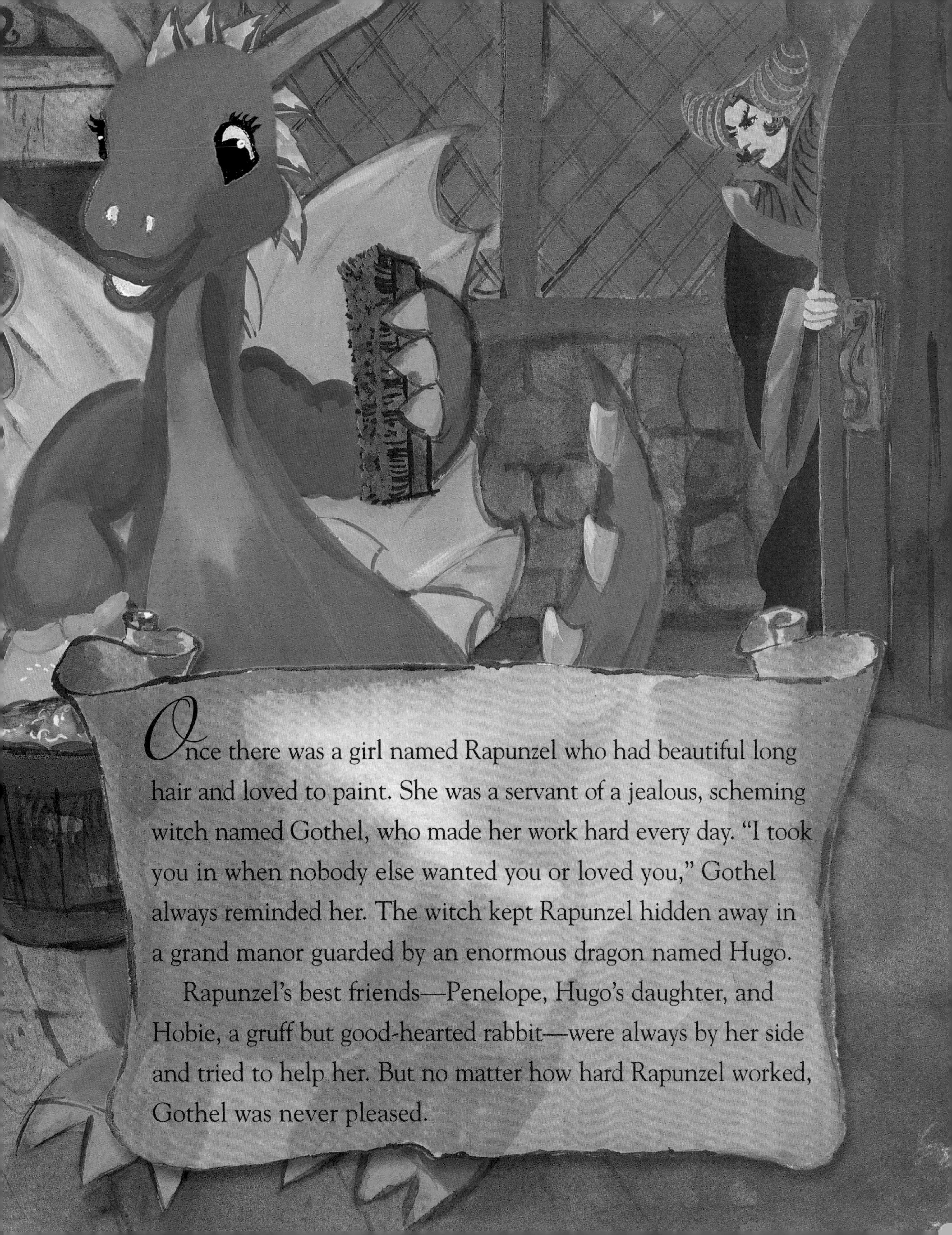

Once there was a girl named Rapunzel who had beautiful long hair and loved to paint. She was a servant of a jealous, scheming witch named Gothel, who made her work hard every day. "I took you in when nobody else wanted you or loved you," Gothel always reminded her. The witch kept Rapunzel hidden away in a grand manor guarded by an enormous dragon named Hugo.

Rapunzel's best friends—Penelope, Hugo's daughter, and Hobie, a gruff but good-hearted rabbit—were always by her side and tried to help her. But no matter how hard Rapunzel worked, Gothel was never pleased.

One day Rapunzel and her friends discovered a secret stairwell beneath the kitchen floor. Curious, they crept down the stairs and found an old wooden chest. Inside the chest was a beautiful silver hairbrush with a poem engraved on the handle:

Constant as the stars above,
Always know that you are loved.
To our daughter, Rapunzel, on her first birthday,
With love forever, Mother and Father.

Rapunzel nearly wept. "Gothel said my parents never loved me . . . that I was left on her doorstep when I was a tiny baby. Why would she have lied to me?"

Suddenly Penelope sneezed and left a smoking hole in the floor—revealing a secret tunnel! Rapunzel crawled through the dark passage till it opened into the forest. Just beyond the forest stood a charming village. And in the distance, a gleaming white castle rose against the sky! Rapunzel was amazed. It was all so beautiful—and so close-by. Why had Gothel told her there was no one living around them for miles?

As Rapunzel walked toward the castle gardens, she saw a young girl start to fall into a pit. Quickly, she ran to the girl and pulled her to safety, but then Rapunzel began to slip into the pit, too! Suddenly, strong arms caught her. She had been rescued by the girl's brother. Rapunzel longed to stay and talk to him, but she feared Gothel would discover her missing. So she ran back into the tunnel without finding out the young man's name. What she did not know was that the girl was a princess and that her brother was a prince—Prince Stefan.

Back at the manor, Gothel's spying ferret, Otto, had already told tales on Rapunzel, and the witch was waiting for her when she returned. "How dare you!" Gothel fumed.

"What are you hiding?" Rapunzel asked her. "You can't keep me locked away from the world forever."

"Watch me!" grinned Gothel. With a magical bolt from her fingertips, she made the door disappear, the stairs vanish, and the wall grow. Gothel then destroyed Rapunzel's easel and paints. The long-haired beauty found herself trapped in a tall tower.

Gothel called Hugo to her. "See to it that she stays put . . . or else," the witch warned him.

Meanwhile, Stefan rode far and wide searching for the beautiful girl who had rescued his sister. He wanted to thank her by inviting her to a masked ball in celebration of his birthday—and he also feared for her safety.

For years his father, King Frederick, had been feuding with King Wilhelm. Stefan didn't know why, but he did know that Wilhelm was preparing to attack the village. The forest was not safe. "I've got to find her!" he declared.

That night Rapunzel dreamed that the handsome young man she had met earlier that day had come to rescue her.

"Rapunzel, Rapunzel, let down your hair!" he called to her. Rapunzel's long hair reached to the ground, and Prince Stefan began to climb up. But Rapunzel's dream turned into a nightmare as Gothel appeared.

Rapunzel woke with a start and looked out the tower window, where Hugo swooped by, eyeing her carefully. She then looked at the hairbrush in her hand and read the poem engraved on the handle. "I will be free," she said determinedly and slipped back into bed. While she slept, a shooting star transformed her hairbrush into a magic paintbrush.

The next morning, Penelope and Hobie brought Rapunzel new paints to cheer her up. It was then that Rapunzel discovered her hairbrush had changed into a paintbrush. Curious, she dipped the brush into the paint and began painting a mural of the garden where she had met Prince Stefan. When she was finished, Rapunzel and her friends were astonished. The painting looked real!

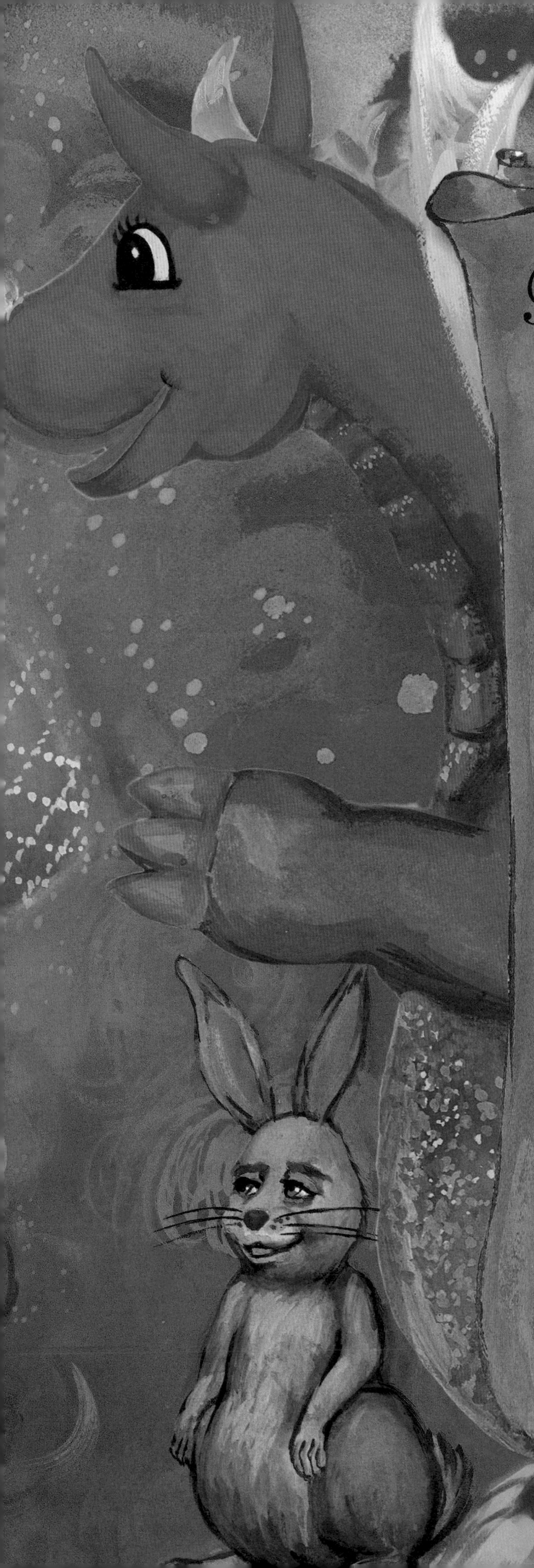

Before he could say another word, Penelope popped through the painting and appeared before Rapunzel and Stefan. "Rapunzel, come quickly! Gothel is heading for the tower," she gasped.

Still unaware of the young man's true identity, Rapunzel promised him she'd attend the ball and hastily said farewell. When she and Penelope were out of his sight, Rapunzel painted a picture of the tower on a garden gate with her magic paintbrush. Then the two friends slipped through the painting and back into the tower before Gothel arrived.

Later that day, Rapunzel began to paint dresses for the ball with her magic paintbrush. Penelope and Hobie helped her design the perfect one. "I feel like a princess!" Rapunzel cried. But she was unaware that Otto had snatched the invitation and had taken it to Gothel.

Gothel was furious when she learned that Rapunzel had escaped again. She stormed into the tower, waving the invitation in the air. "Who gave this to you? Who did you meet?" she demanded.

"Honestly, I-I don't know his name," Rapunzel replied.

"You're lying!" Gothel shouted. Magical bolts flew from her fingertips, cutting off Rapunzel's hair, destroying the painting of the garden, and shattering the magic paintbrush.

Then the witch climbed out the window onto Hugo's back and cast a spell to trap Rapunzel in the tower forever:

Tower, tower, do your part,
Never free your prisoner with a lying heart.
Note that as these words are spoken,
This fearsome spell can never be broken.

An eerie green glint surrounded the tower. Rapunzel was trapped for good without her magic paintbrush.

That evening Gothel went to the masked ball, using Rapunzel's hair to disguise herself. She lured Prince Stefan into the garden, then tore off her mask. "So you're the one meddling in my plans!" she spat.

The prince gasped in horror, "Who are you?"

"I'm the one who's going to teach you to stay away from Rapunzel!" Gothel cackled, throwing magical firebolts at his feet. Prince Stefan dodged the witch's fire, but she chased after him.

Just then, King Wilhelm and his army surrounded King Frederick's castle, surprising all the guests at the ball.

Back at the tower, Penelope had an idea. She and Hobie flew up to the window. "Rapunzel, the spell only traps a prisoner with a lying heart, right? Maybe it won't work on you because your heart is true. You didn't lie to Gothel."

"You could be right," Rapunzel said. And she stepped through the window—right onto the young dragon's back!

Hugo saw that his daughter's friend had a true heart. "Penelope," he said, "take Rapunzel to the ball. I realize now that Gothel is the one who must be stopped."

Penelope took to the air with Rapunzel and Hobie on her back, and they soared across the sky together.

When Rapunzel and her friends arrived at the castle, Rapunzel slipped into the ballroom unnoticed. There, surrounded by guests and soldiers, King Wilhelm and King Frederick were arguing about their long-standing feud.

"You kidnapped my daughter!" King Wilhelm accused King Frederick. "You will pay for—"

"No, I kidnapped her!" Gothel interrupted, making her way through the crowd. She explained she had always loved Wilhelm. But he married another, so in anger she had kidnapped his child and blamed King Frederick to start a feud between the kings and have them destroy each other. "I simply took what was mine," said Gothel.

Rapunzel gasped. She couldn't believe it. King Wilhelm was her father!

Gothel caught sight of Rapunzel among the guests and began to chase her.

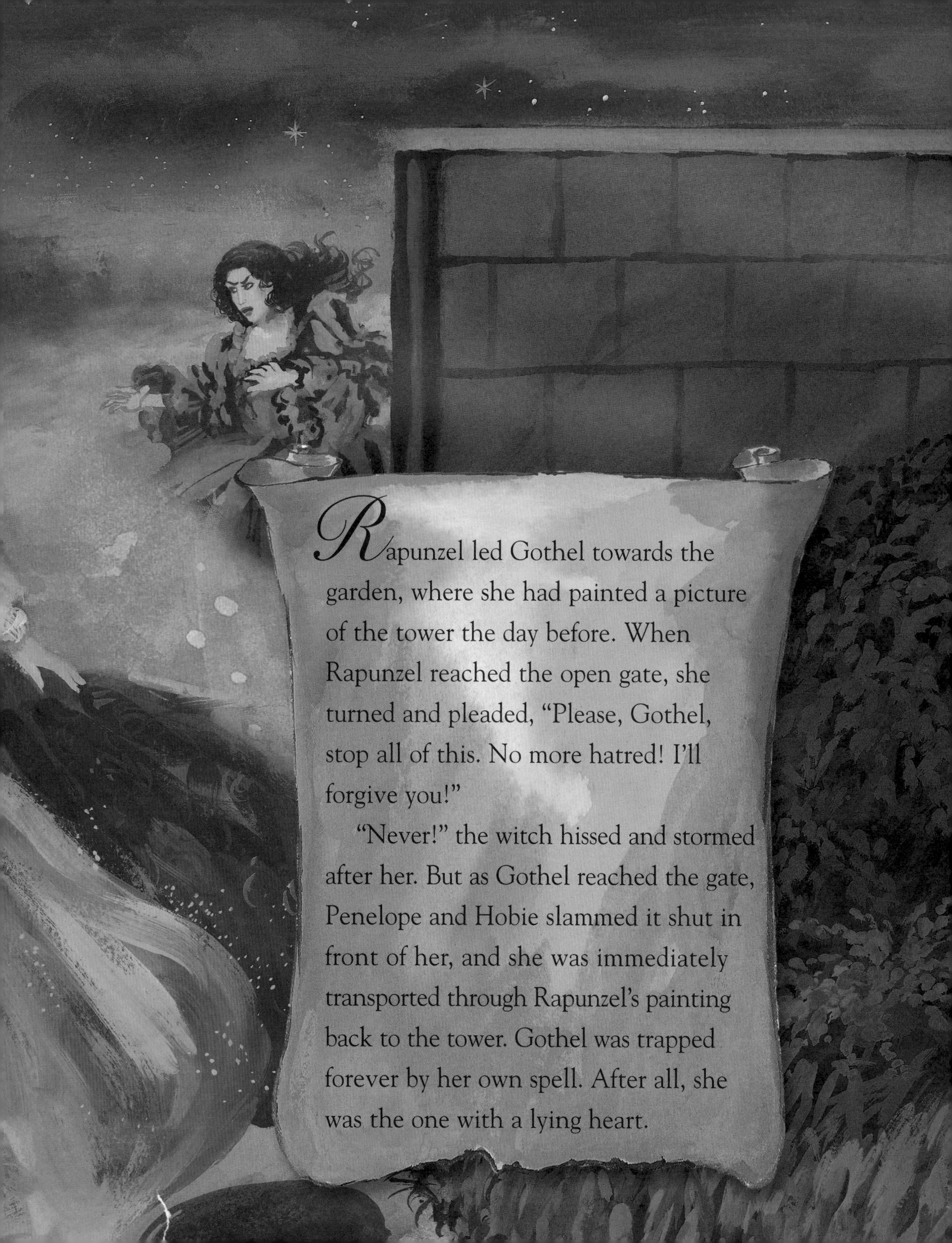

Rapunzel led Gothel towards the garden, where she had painted a picture of the tower the day before. When Rapunzel reached the open gate, she turned and pleaded, "Please, Gothel, stop all of this. No more hatred! I'll forgive you!"

"Never!" the witch hissed and stormed after her. But as Gothel reached the gate, Penelope and Hobie slammed it shut in front of her, and she was immediately transported through Rapunzel's painting back to the tower. Gothel was trapped forever by her own spell. After all, she was the one with a lying heart.

Rapunzel was reunited with her family. "Your mother and I have never stopped thinking about you," King Wilhelm said. "Our love is as constant . . ."

". . . as the stars above," Rapunzel chimed in.

King Wilhelm and King Frederick made their peace and vowed never to fight again. Rapunzel thought she couldn't be happier, until . . .

She married Prince Stefan. They lived happily ever after in their very own castle—where Hobie had all the carrots he could eat and Penelope and Hugo kept the castle warm all year round.

THE END